# GRIMMS' FAIRY TALES

## THE CLASSIC EDITION

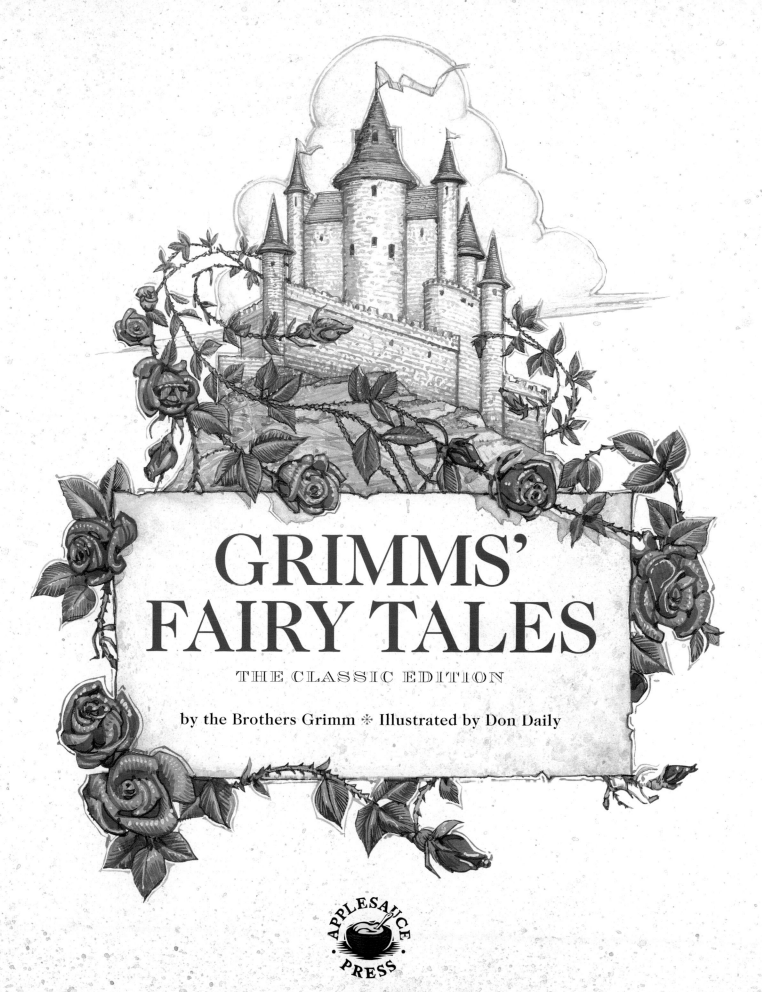

# GRIMMS' FAIRY TALES

## THE CLASSIC EDITION

by the Brothers Grimm ✳ Illustrated by Don Daily

APPLESAUCE PRESS

Kennebunkport, Maine

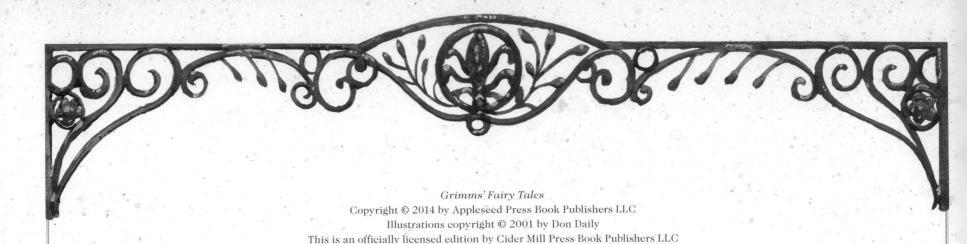

13-Digit ISBN: 978-1-60433-498-2
10-Digit ISBN: 1-60433-498-3

This book may be ordered by mail from the publisher. Please include $4.99 for postage and handling.
Please support your local bookseller first!

Books published by Cider Mill Press Book Publishers are available at special discounts for bulk purchases in the United States by
corporations, institutions, and other organizations. For more information, please contact the publisher.

Applesauce Press is an imprint of
Cider Mill Press Book Publishers
"Where good books are ready for press"
12 Spring Street
PO Box 454
Kennebunkport, Maine 04046

Visit us on the web!
www.cidermillpress.com

Text adapted by Elizabeth Encarnacion
Design by Tango Media
Typography: Chevalier Open DC D & ITC Caslon 224
Printed in China

1 2 3 4 5 6 7 8 9 0
First Edition

To my two wonderful witches Deborah Levine and my wife Renée,
my Hansel and Gretel Conor Foote and Laura Levine, my prince Steve
Gilhool, and last but not least my lovely princess, my daughter Susie.

# Contents

# The Frog Prince

Once upon a time, there lived a king and his beautiful daughter. One fine afternoon the young princess went out to take a walk by herself in the forest near her home. When she came to a cool spring of water, she sat down to rest a while. Her favorite plaything was a golden ball, which she tossed up into the air and caught as it fell. After a time she threw it up so high that she missed catching it, and the ball rolled down and fell into the spring with a splash.

The princess leaned over and looked into the water to find her ball, but the spring was very deep, so deep that she could not see the bottom of it. She began to cry.

As she sobbed, a voice called out to her. "Princess, why do you weep so bitterly?"

She looked around to the spot from which the voice came, and saw a frog sitting on a lily pad. "Was it you that spoke, little frog? I am weeping for my golden ball, which bounced away from me into the water."

"Do not cry," replied the frog, "I can help you. But what will you give me if I bring your plaything up again?"

"What would you like, dear frog?" she asked.

The frog answered, "If you will promise me a kiss, I will swim down below and bring your golden ball to you."

"Oh yes," she said, "I promise, whatever you want, if you will only find my ball." But she thought to herself, "What nonsense this silly frog talks! He lives in the water and croaks with the other frogs, and I will not kiss him!"

After receiving her promise, the frog put his head into the water and sank down, and in a short while came swimming up again with the ball in his mouth and threw it on the grass. The princess was delighted to see her pretty plaything once more, so she picked it up and ran away with it. She soon forgot the poor frog and the promise she had made.

The next day, just as the princess sat down to dinner, she heard a strange noise—*splish splash, splish splash*—as if something wet was coming up the marble staircase. Soon afterward there was a gentle knock at the door, and a little voice called out and said, "Princess, please open the door for me!"

She ran to see who could be at the door, but was quite surprised and frightened to see the frog sitting there.

The king, her father, noticed her reaction and asked her what was wrong.

"There is a disgusting frog at the door!" she said. "Yesterday when I was playing by the spring, my golden ball fell into the water, and this frog fetched it up again because I promised that I would give him a kiss. I never thought that I would have to do it."

The king was an honorable man, and chided his daughter for her thoughtless behavior. "You have given your word and you must keep it."

The princess began to cry, for she was afraid of the cold frog, and did not want to kiss it.

But the king was firm. "What you promised during your time of trouble, you must now perform."

So the princess picked up the frog and gave it a quick kiss before setting it back on the ground. She and her father were shocked when, before their very eyes, the ugly little frog suddenly transformed into a handsome prince!

The prince flexed his hands and stomped his feet as if to confirm that he was back in his human form again. He told the princess and her father that many years ago he had been enchanted by a wicked witch, who had changed him into a frog. Nothing could free him from the evil spell except the kiss of a princess. He had almost lost hope of being transformed until the day when she sat by the spring, playing with her ball.

The princess was embarrassed by her shameful behavior toward the frog, which had almost prevented the prince from breaking the curse. But he assured her that she was forgiven.

"You have broken the cruel charm, and now I have nothing to wish for except that you will marry me. But you must promise me that you will always keep your word. For now you know that things are not always as they seem."

The princess gladly accepted the prince's offer of marriage, and they set out for his kingdom, full of joy and merriment; and there they lived happily ever after.

# Hansel and Gretel

Many years ago near a great forest, there lived a poor woodcutter, his wife, and his two children, Hansel and Gretel. They had very little to eat, and when a great famine fell on the land, the man could not provide his family with enough food.

As the woodcutter prepared for bed one night, he sighed heavily and said to his wife, "What will become of us? How are we to feed our poor children, when we no longer have anything even for ourselves?"

His wife was a cold, uncaring woman who had never liked her stepchildren. "I'll tell you what, husband," answered the woman. "Early tomorrow morning we will take the children out into the forest, where there are berries to eat. We will give each of them a piece of bread for their supper, and then we will leave them there alone."

"No!" said the man, "I could not do such a thing! How could I bear to leave my children alone in the forest?"

"Then we must all four die of hunger. It is the only chance we have to survive," she said, and she gave him no peace until he agreed with her.

After the man reluctantly agreed to his wife's plan, he lamented his decision. "Oh, but I will regret leaving my poor children," he said mournfully.

The two children had not been able to sleep, and had overheard their stepmother's scheme.

"What will become of us? How will we survive?" whispered Hansel.

"Do not worry," Gretel reassured him. "We will figure out some way of finding our way back home."

Early the next morning the stepmother roused them out of bed for an outing in the woods to gather berries. She gave them each a slice of bread to eat for supper.

On the way into the forest Hansel had an idea. He broke his bread into pieces in his pocket, and stooped every now and then to drop a crumb on the ground, being careful not to let his stepmother see what he was doing. Little by little, he threw all the crumbs on the path they traveled.

The stepmother led the children deep into the forest, where they had never been before. After hours of walking she said, "Sit down here and rest. Make yourselves comfortable and sleep for a little while. When I finish gathering the berries, I will come and fetch you."

Exhausted after the morning's hike, Hansel and Gretel fell asleep quickly. Evening came and went, but no one came to fetch the poor children. They did not awake until it was dark night.

"Let's go, Gretel, and find the crumbs of bread that I dropped. They will show us the way home," Hansel said confidently.

They searched and searched but they found no crumbs, for the many birds that had been flying about in the woods and fields had eaten them all up. They walked the whole night and all the next day, but they could not find their way out of the forest, and grew very hungry. Soon they got so tired that their legs would carry them no longer, and they lay down beneath a tree to fall asleep.

The next morning, they awoke to the sound of a bird singing sweetly. When it had finished its song, it spread its wings and flew away before them, and they followed it until they reached a little cottage. As they approached the house, they saw that it was built of gingerbread and covered with icing and candy, with windows of clear sugar.

"The house is made of food!" said Hansel. "We can eat it and have a good meal." He reached up and broke a piece off the roof to see how it tasted, while Gretel stepped up to the window and nibbled at the panes.

A soft voice cried, "Nibble, nibble, like a mouse, who is nibbling at my house?"

Suddenly the door opened, and a very old woman with a cane came creeping out. Hansel and Gretel were so terribly frightened that they dropped the food they had in their hands.

The old woman looked them over, and then nodded her head kindly and said, "Oh, you dear children, what has brought you here?" Hansel and Gretel told the old woman how their stepmother had left them deep in the forest and how they had not been able to find the breadcrumbs that were to guide them home.

"Poor dears! Do come in, and stay with me. No harm shall happen to you here." The old woman took them both by the hand and led them into her little house.

Soon she was feeding them a delicious meal of milk and pancakes with sugar, apples, and nuts. After dinner, she tucked Hansel and Gretel into a bed covered with clean white linen. After sleeping in the forest for several nights, the children felt as though they were in heaven.

While the children lay sleeping peacefully, the old woman watched over them, her kind eyes hardening into an evil expression as she dropped her innocent disguise. The old woman had only pretended to be kind. In reality, she was a wicked witch who liked to eat little children. Seeing Hansel and Gretel's round, rosy cheeks, she said to herself, "What a fine feast I shall have!"

She grasped Hansel with her withered hands and shut him up in a little cage, locking the door. Although he screamed loudly and fought to escape, it was of no use.

Gretel awoke, but Hansel was already locked away. Seeing her stir, the witch cried, "Get up, you lazy thing! Fetch some water and cook something good for your brother to eat. When he is fat enough, I will eat him."

Gretel cried bitterly, but the wicked witch forced the little girl to do as she said. And so the best food was cooked for poor Hansel, but Gretel got nothing but crab-shells.

Every morning the woman came to the cage and said, "Hansel, stretch out your finger so I may feel whether you are getting fat enough."

Hansel, however, cleverly stretched out a little stick he had found in the cage. The old woman, who had very bad eyesight, felt it and thought it was Hansel's finger, and was astonished that he did not get any fatter.

After a while, the witch lost all her patience and would not wait any longer. "Gretel," she cried to the girl, "go light the fire. Today I will cook your brother, whether he is fat or lean."

Gretel reluctantly obeyed. Once the fire's flames were darting from the oven, the witch pulled poor Gretel over toward the oven door. "Crawl in," said the witch, "and tell me if it is properly heated."

But Gretel guessed at the witch's trick. She knew that once she was inside, the witch would shut the oven door and eat her, too. So Gretel replied, "I am sorry, but I do not think I am small enough to get through the oven door. Are you sure I will fit?"

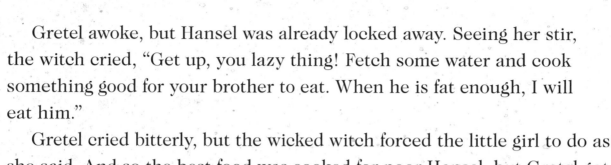

"Silly goose," said the old woman, "The door is big enough for you. Just look, I could even get in myself!" and she put her head into the oven to demonstrate.

As the witch leaned into the oven, Gretel gave her a hard push, so that the witch fell right in. Then she shut the iron door and fastened the bolt.

The witch begged Gretel to let her out, and promised she wouldn't hurt the two children, but Gretel ignored her and went to let her brother out of the cage.

"Hansel, we are saved! The old witch is dead!" Gretel called to him as she unlocked the door. Hansel sprang out of the cage and hugged his sister. They were so glad to be saved from the witch that they danced around with joy.

But later, as they walked outside, they realized they were not yet out of harm's way. They were still lost in the forest, and could not find their way home.

Just then, they heard the whistle of a songbird. Looking up, they saw the same little bird that had guided them to the witch's cottage.

"Dear children, I am so thankful to you for breaking the witch's spell and allowing me to fly freely!" How can I ever repay you?"

"We do not know the way home," Gretel said. "Can you show us the path to our little cottage?"

"Certainly," the bird said. "Just follow me, and you'll be home before long."

After they had followed the bird for a time, the forest began to seem more and more familiar to them. When they finally saw their father cutting wood outside his cottage, they ran to him and threw themselves into their father's arms.

"Hansel and Gretel! Oh, my dear children. I have not known one happy hour since you have been gone," he said.

He then told them that their uncaring stepmother had died while they were in the forest, and that he had deeply regretted allowing her to take them away.

"I will never let anyone separate us again," he promised.

Reunited at last, all of their sorrows were at an end, and they lived together in perfect happiness.

# Rapunzel

There once lived a man and his wife who had long wished for a child. At the back of their house there was a little window that overlooked a splendid garden full of the finest vegetables and most beautiful flowers. A high wall surrounded it, and no one dared to go inside because it belonged to a powerful witch who was dreaded by all the world.

One day the woman was looking down into the garden when she saw a patch planted with the most beautiful rapunzel lettuce. It looked so fresh and green that she had the greatest desire to eat some. This went on for days, and she grew weak and miserable because she knew she could not have the witch's lettuce.

Her husband worried about her. One evening, he climbed over the wall into the witch's garden, hastily picked a handful of the lettuce, and took it to his wife. She made a salad of it at once, and ate it with much relish. However, the next day she longed for it three times as much as before.

Her husband returned to the garden the next evening, but when he had clambered down the wall he was terribly afraid, for he saw the witch standing before him.

"How dare you climb over into my garden like a thief, and steal my lettuce!" she said. "You will suffer for it!"

The man begged the witch for mercy and explained the reason for his nighttime visit. "My wife saw your beautiful lettuce from the window, and felt such a longing for it that she would have died if she had not gotten some to eat."

The witch allowed her anger to be softened, and said to him, "If what you say is true, you may have as much of my lettuce as you like, on one condition—you must give me the child that your wife will soon bring into the world. It will be well treated, and I will care for it like a mother."

In his terror, the man agreed to give up his first-born child. Later that year when his wife gave birth to a child, the witch appeared at once, gave the baby girl the name of Rapunzel, and took it away with her.

Rapunzel grew into the most beautiful child beneath the sun, with magnificent long hair, fine as spun gold. When she was twelve years old, the witch shut her into a tower deep in the forest. The tower had neither stairs nor door, but right at the top was a little window. When the witch wanted to go in, she placed herself beneath it and cried,

"Rapunzel, Rapunzel, let down your hair!"

When Rapunzel heard the voice of the witch, she unfastened her braided tresses, wound them around one of the hooks of the window above, and then lowered it out the window so the witch could climb up. The witch and Rapunzel lived like this for several years. Rapunzel was very lonely, for she could not escape the tower and had no visitors but the witch.

But then one day, a prince rode through the forest and heard a voice singing so sweetly that he followed it to the tower. Looking up, he could see Rapunzel, who was trying to amuse herself with sweet songs.

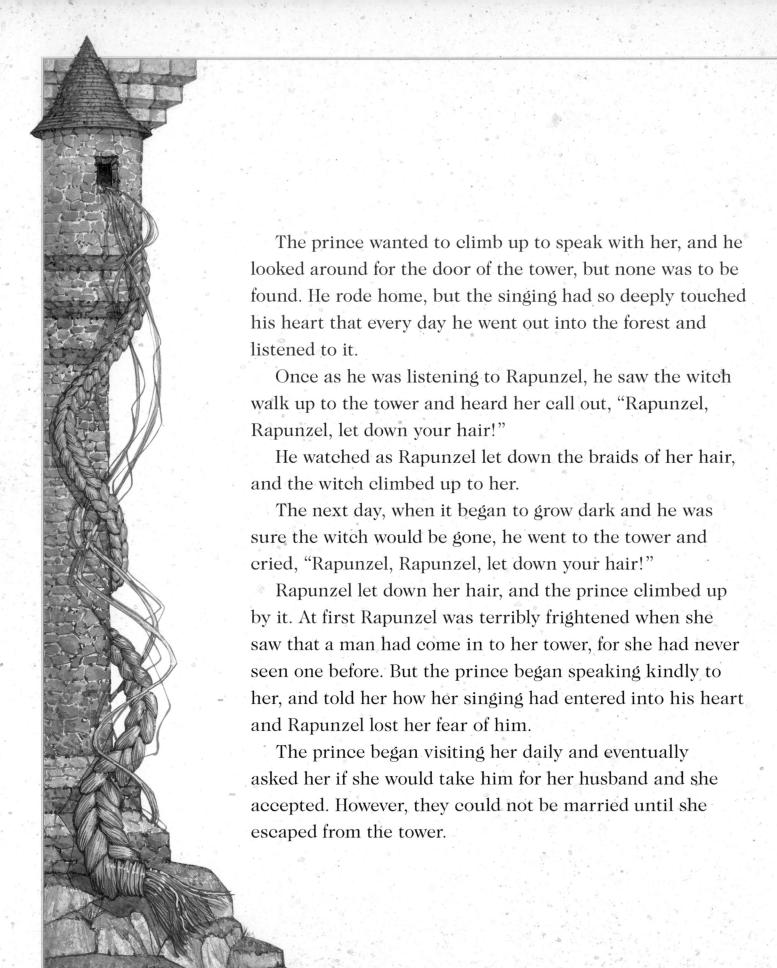

The prince wanted to climb up to speak with her, and he looked around for the door of the tower, but none was to be found. He rode home, but the singing had so deeply touched his heart that every day he went out into the forest and listened to it.

Once as he was listening to Rapunzel, he saw the witch walk up to the tower and heard her call out, "Rapunzel, Rapunzel, let down your hair!"

He watched as Rapunzel let down the braids of her hair, and the witch climbed up to her.

The next day, when it began to grow dark and he was sure the witch would be gone, he went to the tower and cried, "Rapunzel, Rapunzel, let down your hair!"

Rapunzel let down her hair, and the prince climbed up by it. At first Rapunzel was terribly frightened when she saw that a man had come in to her tower, for she had never seen one before. But the prince began speaking kindly to her, and told her how her singing had entered into his heart and Rapunzel lost her fear of him.

The prince began visiting her daily and eventually asked her if she would take him for her husband and she accepted. However, they could not be married until she escaped from the tower.

"Each time you visit me," she said, "bring a length of silk and I will weave a ladder with it. When that is ready, I will climb down, and you will take me away on your horse."

The witch knew nothing of all of this until one day Rapunzel said, without thinking, "Mother, how is it that you climb up here so slowly, while the prince is with me in a moment?"

"Oh wicked child," cried the witch. "What is this I hear? I thought I had hidden you from all the world, and yet you have deceived me."

In her anger she seized Rapunzel's beautiful hair and cut it off, dropping the lovely braids on the ground. The witch took Rapunzel out of the tower and moved her to a faraway place, where she lived in grief and misery.

On the same day that she cast out Rapunzel, the witch fastened the braids of hair that she had cut off to the hook of the window, and when the prince came and cried, "Rapunzel, Rapunzel, let down your hair," she let the hair down.

The prince ascended, but he did not find his dearest Rapunzel above. Instead he came face to face with the witch, who glared at him and cried mockingly, "Aha! You came for your Rapunzel, but she is lost to you. I have hidden her away and you will see her no more."

The prince was beside himself with grief. In his despair he leapt out the window and fell from the tower. He escaped with his life, but the thorns into which he fell damaged his eyes horribly. Blinded, he wandered through the forest, mourning for the loss of his dearest love.

One day, many years later, the prince unknowingly came to the lonely, deserted place where Rapunzel lived. He heard a gentle voice, and it seemed so familiar to him that he walked toward it. When he approached, Rapunzel recognized her lost love and wrapped him in her arms and wept. When her tears touched his eyes, they cleared and he could once again see.

Reunited with his love, the prince took Rapunzel to his kingdom, where he was received with great joy. They married and lived for a long time afterward, happy and contented.

# The Old Woman in the Forest

In days past, a poor peasant girl was once traveling and found herself lost in a great forest. She began to weep bitterly, and said, "What can a poor girl like me do now? I do not know how to get out of the forest, so I will certainly starve."

The maiden walked around and looked for a road, but could find none. As night fell, she seated herself under a tree and resolved to sit waiting there until something happened.

After she had rested there for a while, a white dove came flying to her with a little golden key in its mouth. It put the little key in her hand, and said, "Do you see that great tree? On the tree is a door with a little lock. It opens with this tiny key, and inside you will find food enough, and suffer no more hunger."

The maiden went to the tree and opened it, and found milk in a little dish, and white bread to break into it, so that she could eat her fill. When she was satisfied, she said, "It is now the time when the hens go to roost. I am so tired that I wish I could go to bed too."

Then the dove flew to her again and brought another golden key in its bill. It said, "Open that tree there, and you will find a bed." So she opened it and found a beautiful white bed, and she lay down and slept.

In the morning the dove came for the third time, and again brought a little key, and said, "Open that tree there, and you will find clothes." And when she opened it, she found garments lined with gold and jewels, more splendid than those of any princess.

So she lived there in the woods for some time, and the dove came every day and provided her with all she needed, and it was a quiet, good life.

One morning, however, the dove came and said, "Will you do a favor for me?"

"You have done so much for me," said the maiden. "I will do whatever you wish."

Then the little dove said, "I will guide you to a small house. Enter it, and inside an old woman will be sitting by the fire and will say, 'Good day.' But you must give her no answer, no matter what she does. Walk by her to the closed door. It leads into a room that contains rings of all kinds and sizes, magnificent ones with shining stones. Leave them where they are, and seek out the plain one among them, and bring it here to me as quickly as you can."

The young woman went to the little house and entered the front door. By the fire sat an old woman who stared when she saw the maiden, and said, "Good day, my child." The maiden gave the old woman no answer, and walked past her to the closed door.

"Where are you going?" cried the old woman, and seized her by the gown. "This is my house. No one may enter that room without my permission."

But the maiden was silent. She pulled away from the old woman and went straight into the back room. An enormous quantity of rings gleamed and glittered before her eyes on the table. She turned them over and looked for the plain one, but could not find it. While she was searching, she noticed the old woman stealing away with a birdcage. So the maiden followed her and took the cage out of her hand. When the maiden raised the cage up and looked inside, she discovered a bird with the plain ring in its bill. She took the ring, and ran quite joyously home with it.

The maiden thought the little white dove would come and get the ring, but it did not. As she waited for the dove, she leaned against a tree, which felt soft and flexible, as if it were letting its branches down. And suddenly the branches twined around her, and were two arms, and when she looked around, the tree had become a handsome man.

He embraced and kissed her heartily, and said, "You have delivered me from the power of the old woman, who is a wicked witch. She had changed me into a tree, and left me unable to speak or move. Every day for a few hours I was a white dove, and could fly around and sing songs, but as long as she possessed the ring I could not regain my human form."

Then his servants and his horses, who had likewise been changed into trees, were freed from the enchantment also and stood beside him. And he led them all home to his kingdom, for he was a King's son. The prince and maiden soon married, and lived happily ever after.

# Brier Rose

Once upon a time there lived a king and queen who had plenty of money, and plenty of fine clothes to wear, and plenty of good things to eat and drink. Yet despite their many blessings, they were very disappointed, for they had no children.

One day as the Queen was walking by the side of the river, a frog crept onto a lily pad and said to her, "Your wish shall be fulfilled; before a year has gone by, you shall have a daughter."

What the frog had said came true, and within a year the Queen had given birth to a baby girl. The King and Queen were so delighted they could not contain their joy. They ordered a great feast and invited not only their relations, friends, and neighbors, but also the Wise Women, in order that they might be kind and well-disposed toward the child. There were thirteen Wise Women in the kingdom, but as the King had only twelve golden plates for them to eat out of, one of them was left without an invitation.

The feast was held with much rejoicing, and when it came to an end, the Wise Women bestowed their magical gifts upon the baby. One gave virtue, another beauty, a third riches, and so on with everything in the world that one can wish for.

When eleven of them had made their promises, suddenly the thirteenth charged in. Furious at being slighted by the royal family, she pointed at the princess and cried with a loud voice, "In her fifteenth year, the King's daughter shall prick herself with a spindle, and fall down dead." Then she stormed out of the great hall, leaving them all shocked in her wake.

The twelfth Wise Woman, whose good wish still remained unspoken, came forward. She could not undo the evil sentence, but she could soften it. She said, "When the princess pricks her finger on her fifteenth birthday, she shall not die but instead fall into a deep sleep of a hundred years."

The King hoped to save his dear child from the threatened evil, so he gave orders that every spindle in the whole kingdom should be burnt. As the princess grew up, the gifts of the first eleven Wise Women were fulfilled, for the princess was so beautiful, good-natured, generous, and wise that everyone who met her was bound to love her.

It happened that on the very day when the princess turned fifteen years old, the King and Queen were not at home, and she was left in the palace quite alone. So the princess explored around the palace by herself, looking into all the rooms and bedchambers, until at last she came to an old tower. Curious, she climbed up the narrow, winding staircase and reached a little door. As she reached out her hand, the door sprang open. There in a little room sat an old woman with a spindle, busily spinning her flax.

"Good day," said the princess. "What are you doing there?"

"I am spinning," said the old woman, nodding her head.

"What sort of thing is that, that rattles around so merrily?" asked the girl, reaching her hand toward the spindle. But as soon as she touched it, she pricked her finger and immediately fell down upon the bed that stood there, falling into a deep sleep.

This sleep extended over the whole palace; the King and Queen, who had just come home and entered the great hall, fell asleep, and the whole of the court with them. The horses, too, went to sleep in the stable, the dogs in the yard, the pigeons upon the roof, the flies on the wall. Even the fire that was flaming on the hearth became quiet and slept.

Around the castle grew a hedge of thorns, which every year became higher. Eventually the brier hedge grew all over the castle so that none of it could be seen, not even the flag upon the roof. But the story of the beautiful sleeping Brier Rose, as the princess was called, was told throughout the country. From time to time, princes tried to get through the brier hedge into the castle, but they always found it impossible, for the thorns held fast together.

After many, many years, another prince came to that country. He met an old man who told him the story of the brier hedge, and how a castle stood behind it in which a wonderfully beautiful princess named Brier Rose had been asleep for a hundred years, along with all her court. The old man also told of the many princes who had tried unsuccessfully to get through the thorny hedge. But the prince said, "I am not afraid, I will go and save the princess Brier Rose."

The prince set out for the palace on the very day the hundred years of slumber had been completed. Thus, when the prince came near to the brier hedge, he found nothing but large and beautiful flowers, which parted from each other and let him pass unhurt. In the castle's yard, he saw the horses and the spotted hounds lying asleep; on the roof sat the pigeons with their heads under their wings. When he entered the great hall, he saw the whole of the court lying asleep, and up by the throne lay the King and Queen.

The prince continued deeper into the palace, and everything was so still that he could hear every breath he drew. At last he climbed the steps to the tower, and opened the door of the little room where Brier Rose was sleeping.

There she lay, so beautiful that
he could not turn his eyes away,
so he leaned over and gently gave
her a kiss. The moment he kissed
her, Brier Rose began to open
her eyes, awakening with a smile
for the prince. Then they went
down to the great hall together,
where the King, the Queen, and
the whole court were waking up
and looking at each other in great
astonishment. The horses stood up
and shook themselves, the hounds
jumped up and wagged their tails,
the pigeons flew into the air, the
flies on the wall buzzed about, and
the fire in the kitchen once again
flickered and cooked the meat as
the kingdom came back to life.

Soon thereafter, the wedding of the prince and Brier Rose was celebrated throughout the kingdom, and they lived happily together to the end of their days.